DISCARDED
SOUTH RUTLAND ELEMENTARY

SOUTH RUTLAND
ELEMENTARY LIBRARY

Children of the World

Kuntai

A Masai Child

By Muriel Nicolotti

BLACKBIRCH PRESS
An imprint of Thomson Gale, a part of The Thomson Corporation

Detroit • New York • San Francisco • San Diego • New Haven, Conn. • Waterville, Maine • London • Munich

© Éditions PEMF, 2000

First published by PEMF in France as *Kuntai, enfant Massaï*.

First published in North America in 2005 by Thomson Gale.

Thomson and Star Logo are trademarks and Gale and Blackbirch Press are registered trademarks used herein under license.

For more information, contact
Blackbirch Press
27500 Drake Rd.
Farmington Hills, MI 48331-3535
Or you can visit our Internet site at http://www.gale.com

ALL RIGHTS RESERVED.
No part of this work covered by the copyright hereon may be reproduced or used in any form or by any means—graphic, electronic, or mechanical, including photocopying, recording, taping, Web distribution or information storage retrieval systems—without the written permission of the publisher.

Every effort has been made to trace the owners of copyrighted material.

Photo Credits: All photos © Muriel Nicolotti except pages 6 (bottom), 8 (bottom), 17 (left) © Royalty Free/CORBIS; page 10 (left), Corel Corporation; Table of Contents collage: EXPLORER/Boutin (upper left); François Goalec (upper middle and right); Muriel Nicolotti (bottom left); CIRIC/Michel Gauvry (bottom middle); CIRIC/Pascal Deloche (bottom right).

LIBRARY OF CONGRESS CATALOGING-IN-PUBLICATION DATA

Nicolotti, Muriel.
  Kuntai : a Masai child / by Muriel Nicolotti.
    p. cm. — (Children of the world)
  ISBN 1-4103-0290-3 (alk. paper)
  1. Masai (African people)—Social life and customs—Juvenile literature. 2. Children—Kenya—Social life and customs—Juvenile literature. 3. Children—Tanzania—Social life and customs—Juvenile literature. 4. Kenya—Social life and customs—Juvenile literature. 5. Tanzania—Social life and customs—Juvenile literature. I. Title. II. Series: Children of the world (Blackbirch Press)

DT433.545.M33N53 2005
967.62'004965—dc22

2005000701

Printed in the United States of America
10 9 8 7 6 5 4 3 2 1

Contents

Facts About the Land of the Masai 5
Masai Country. 6
Protecting the Elephants 8
The Masai. 10
Kuntai's Home 12
In the Grazing Lands. 14
Evening in the Boma 16
Food 18
Education 20
Ceremonies. 22
Other Books in the Series 24

Facts About the Land of the Masai

Agriculture: cattle raising
Languages: Maa, Swahili
Natural Resources: land for raising cattle
Population: 300,000
Religion: Indigenous Polytheism
Tribes: The Arusha, the Baraguyu, the Kisong, the Purko, and the Samburu
Where: The Masai live along each side of the border between Kenya and Tanzania, including the reserves of Masai Mara and Amboseli in Kenya. They also live in reserves of the Serengeti and Lake Natron and the crater of Ngorongoro in Tanzania at the foot of Mount Kilimanjaro.

Masai Country

Kuntai is nine years old. He lives with his parents near Masai Mara wildlife reserve in Kenya.

Right: Kuntai

Masai Mara is a national park. More than 3 million animals make their home here, including rhinoceroses, lions, cape buffaloes, elephants, giraffes, wildebeests, gazelles, and zebras. The Masai graze their cattle in the reserve.

Right: Masai fear cape buffalo the most because they are unpredictable. When they charge, they often kill.

Below left: A rhinoceros grazes at Masai Mara.

Below right: Lions often attack the Masai's herds.

Protecting the Elephants

In the reserve, elephants are protected from poachers. These hunters kill elephants for their ivory tusks.

Elephants like these in the Masai Mara wildlife preserve are protected from poachers.

Because the elephants are kept in the reserve, they cannot migrate the whole length of Africa, as they used to do. So, the animals have become too numerous. They have destroyed many trees in the savanna.

Above: An elephant and her calf.

Left: Giraffes feed on the highest levels of trees.

The Masai

The Masai were once proud and fierce warriors. They waged many battles to conquer the great plains of Kenya and Tanzania.

They can be identified by their long red capes and their spears and shields.

A young Masai girl wears many necklaces and beaded jewelry.

Kuntai's Home

Kuntai lives in a boma, or village. The Masai build their homes all in the same way. Each house has three rooms. One room is for guests, one is for the animals, and one is a main room where there are sleeping mats and a cooking fire.

Above: Kuntai stands in front of the door to his house.

Left: This house in Kuntai's village is under construction.

The Masai do not use furniture. Adults and children sleep on mats right on the floor. The walls and the roof are made of interwoven branches. Then they are covered with a mix of dried grass and cow manure.

Kuntai's mother must regularly patch the roof, because it dries out and cracks in the sun.

Below: The village has a circular shape. It is surrounded by a barrier of thorny branches that protect the people and livestock from wild animals.

Kuntai's mother fixes the roof.

In the Grazing Lands

Each family owns a dozen cows, goats, and sheep. Each animal is branded with a sign that identifies to whom it belongs.

The Masai men take their herds into the animal reserve to graze for several days. Just before they leave, they go into the bush to eat a sheep roasted over an open fire.

A herd of cattle crosses the savanna in the midst of zebras and wildebeest.

The herd leaves for the grazing lands.

The oldest Masai warrior guides the herds across the savanna. Kuntai and his friends follow along for a few miles (kilometers), but soon they must go back to take care of the goats and sheep.

The young boys take care of the smaller animals. When the boys grow up, they will herd the cattle.

Kuntai cradles one of his goats.

Evening in the Boma

In the evening, after the return of the herds, the chiefs discuss where to graze the cattle the next day.

The women make beaded necklaces and bracelets for the whole family.

Kuntai likes to watch how jewelry is made.

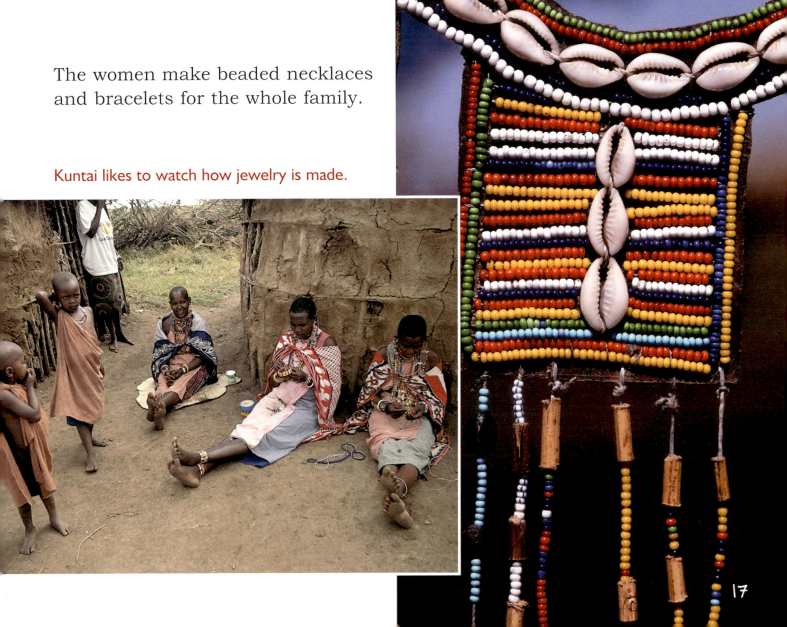

Food

To make the evening meal, the women take some blood from the young bulls. A bowl of blood mixed with milk is the basic food of the Masai.

Kuntai checks on the goat that is going to have a baby. He wants to make sure that she is well.

Kuntai is responsible for the goat that is soon to have a baby.

Education

Kuntai, like all Masai children, does not go to school. The elders teach them all that a Masai needs to know. They learn how to recognize and take care of plants and animals. They also learn good manners and a history of the people.

The women teach the children to stay away from the fireplace. The Masai believe that evil spirits live there.

Kuntai is still a layonis, or child. In a few years, when he is about fourteen, he will become a morane, or warrior. He will leave his family to go live with other boys his age in a manyata, a village built in the bush.

Above: Elders teach the children until they are fourteen.

Left: A morane braids his hair, which has been coated with a mixture of ochre and fat.

There, an elder will teach him to use weapons, memorize war chants, and learn traditional dances.

The boys will grow their hair long and will braid it carefully.

Ceremonies

When a morane has completed his apprenticeship to become a warrior, he can go back to the village, get married, and take care of a herd of cattle. His graduation is celebrated for a whole week.

During the dances, the Masai cover their bodies with ochre and put ostrich feathers around their heads.

In one of the dances, the men walk in a single file and imitate a snake. The women and children follow, making their heavy beaded necklaces bounce as they go.

The morane cuts his long braided hair and puts on traditional clothes decorated with beads.

During the jumping contest, the men face the singers and jump as high as they can. They keep their feet together and their arms at their sides.

SOUTH RUTLAND ELEMENTARY LIBRARY

Other Books in the Series

Arafat: A Child of Tunisia
Asha: A Child of the Himalayas
Avinesh: A Child of the Ganges
Ballel: A Child of Senegal
Basha: A Hmong Child
Frederico: A Child of Brazil

Ituko: An Inuit Child
Kradji: A Child of Cambodia
Leila: A Tuareg Child
Madhi: A Child of Egypt
Thanassis: A Child of Greece
Tomasino: A Child of Peru

SOUTH RUTLAND
ELEMENTARY LIBRARY